INTO THE DARKNESS

DARKNESS I

NORA ASH

This is a work of fiction. Any and all likeness to trademarks, corporations or persons, dead or alive, is purely coincidental.

ABOUT THE AUTHOR

Nora Ash writes thrilling romance and sexy paranormal fantasy.

Visit her website to learn more about her upcoming books.

WWW.NORA-ASH.COM

ONE

The one good thing about living in a city that boasts a crime rate a good forty percent above the national average is that there's always something to report on, even for a small-time blogger like myself.

Granted, I could have done without having my late-night coffee run intercepted by an armed robbery, but at least it would give me something to write about. If I didn't get myself shot, of course.

My heart pounded in my throat as I pressed my cheek against the floor. From my low vantage point, I couldn't see much other than the robbers' boots and cargo pants, but I could hear their demands clear as day.

"Hurry up and empty that register!" one of them snarled at the poor kid behind the counter. "Or you'll get a head full of lead."

"And throw in a cappuccino," the guy casually pointing his gun toward me and the other customers cowering on the floor added.

Who the heck asked for a cup of coffee in the middle of a

robbery? Surprise—and possibly stupidity—made me twist my neck and look up. My efforts were for nothing; he was wearing a mask, blending into the anonymous masses of wrongdoers littering the seedy underbelly of St. Anthony.

"What are you looking at, bitch?" Mr. Cappuccino growled, and with an unpleasant drop in my stomach, I realized that the big gun was now pointed directly at my face.

I gaped up at him like a fish on land, my brain taking a complete timeout instead of doing something useful like, I dunno, *not staring at the man with the gun.*

He pulled his upper lip back in a snarl, displaying crooked yellow teeth, and I had a second's worth of thinking *stereotype much?* before my brain got up to speed.

"I'm sorry!" I gasped. The barrel seemed so dark, but I didn't have time to look back down to the floor before the window by the door exploded.

Both robbers spun around, whipping their guns with them to point at the figure now standing in the middle of the broken glass.

"Fuck!"

I craned my neck to see what had made Mr. Cappuccino's partner shout, and couldn't help the involuntary intake of breath when I got a closer look at the newcomer.

Charcoal and crimson high-tech fabric covered his strong, chiseled body all the way up to his neck, and the top half of his face was covered in a similarly-colored leather mask. He was tall and lean, and his eyes glowed an unnatural blue, highlighting his perfect mouth and strong jaw. I knew that man. Hell, everyone in St. Anthony knew him.

"Really, a coffee shop?" He folded his arms across his chest, surveying his surroundings. His gaze skimmed over my awkwardly sprawled form to the three other customers huddled somewhere behind me. "I mean, a bank or a jeweler's, sure, but a *coffee shop?*"

The robbers' reply was to fire their weapons.

My brain finally turned on, and I did the only reasonable thing there is to do when someone's firing automatic guns around you–-I dove for cover underneath the nearest table and saw the other customers and the poor employee do the same out of the corner of my eye. From my hiding place, I had a near-perfect view of the newcomer as he darted past the flying bullets with superhuman agility and leapt over the counter.

Lightning was what he went by in the news and on social media, more because of his supernatural speed than actually being able to shoot lightning—though I wasn't completely certain that some of the superhumans walking among us weren't able to do that, too.

I'd seen pictures and video clips of him—and a few of the other masked *supers* we called heroes—but I'd never been this close to one before. Despite the flying bullets and shattering furniture, I whipped out my phone and pressed "record" while I tried to creep out far enough from my protective shelter to get a decent angle, without losing a hand to stray bullets.

It quickly became evident that Lightning was just playing with the two unlucky robbers. He dodged bullets as if they were nothing more than annoying flies, popping up behind one and then the other opponent to give him a quick smack or a light shove to make them stumble or lose their aim. After a few minutes of impressive acrobatics, he finally got down to business. He jumped on top of the counter and easily twisted his body mid-air to avoid an attack before hitting first one guy square in the jaw with a kick, and then the other in the neck. Both dropped to the floor like two sacks of potatoes, their guns clattering beside them.

Lightning smiled and placed his hands on his narrow hips, looking oddly like a housewife who'd just finished sweeping the floor. "You can come out of your hidey-holes now, good people," he said. "They'll be out for..."

The moment his eyes locked on me—and the phone I was still using to record him with—he paused, a mixture of amusement and surprise flickering in his glowing blue eyes.

"Did you just video that? Through all the gunfire?"

I blinked up at him. Did he just... speak *to me? Me?*

I could tell I was staring mutely for an inappropriate amount of time when he smirked beneath his mask, and I felt a furious blush heat up my face.

"Yeah-huh," I managed to stutter.

He easily jumped off the counter and walked toward me in a smooth, confident stride, and I have no idea how I didn't drop my phone.

I stared up at him, distantly aware of my mouth hanging open at being so close to a superhuman. A superhuman who was currently smiling down at my awkwardly kneeling figure half-hidden underneath a café table.

And then it dawned on me. I had his full attention, if only for a short moment. Uploading a video of *Lightning* in action would boost my meager blog traffic for sure, but if I could snag an interview? That would give me so many views I might actually be able to both pay my bills *and* pay off some of my credit card debt!

"Could I ask you a few questions?" I blurted out, opting for the direct approach rather than to risk losing my nerve.

His smile turned impossible brighter, exposing his even, white teeth and a dimple over the left corner of his mouth. In other words, he was exactly as swoon-worthy in real life as in his pictures. "Sure thing, darling."

I tried to ignore my flushing cheeks and instead did my best to put on my professional persona. Not that a small-time cultural blogger like myself could be considered overly professional on the best of days, let alone while crouching on the floor in the middle of a crime scene.

With the support of the chair I'd hidden behind, I climbed out from under the table. The top of my head still only came up to about his shoulders, but at least it was easier to aim the camera at his face now.

"Um, thank you. So, how did you know there was a robbery taking place here?" I tried my best to compose my face into a professional mask, but judging from the heat of it, it was still beet red. "Do you hack into security systems?"

Lightning sighed melodramatically and brushed a hand across the top of his head, still shielded by the leather mask. "And here I thought you were going to ask me about how much protein I eat every day. Or perhaps my workout routine. I didn't take you for such a *serious reporter*."

Something about the way he emphasized "serious reporter" made me bristle. He might as well have been doing air quotes. And okay, so I wasn't exactly employed by a big TV station... or anywhere, actually. And I knew my stuttering and blushing probably didn't make me seem super experienced, but still. I was proud of my work. Most of the time, anyway.

"Well, I am," I snapped. "I am Kathryn Smith, author of the cultural blog 'The Dark City.' It's not a big site, but it *is* serious. Now, how do you know when people are in need of a hero, Mr. Lightning? I'm sure it's something we all would like to know."

"I'm sure it is, darling. I'm just not overly inclined to share. Can't have the bad guys catching on, you see." He offered me a cheeky wink that somehow took the edge off the blow-off. "But I think St. Anthony's finest might be on their way now, so if you want a final question in before I gotta run, best get it out now."

About a million questions milled around at the forefront of my mind. There were so many things I'd fantasized about asking a superhuman, if I ever got in the position to ask one. The problem was that most of those questions were ones that everyone wanted to ask—and no one ever got the answer to. Like, *"Why do you have these powers?" "What exactly can you do?"* and, *"what's your real name?"* Given Lightning's less than willing attitude toward providing some chubby girl he'd just happened to save from being shot dead with details of how he'd managed to do just that, I didn't have high hopes that he'd cave and spill his deepest secrets to my cell phone camera.

I stared up at the masked man, willing my brain to produce a substantial question he wasn't going to shoot down straight away.

"Does being a vigilante with a secret identity make it hard to keep meaningful relationships?"

A self-satisfied smile spread on my face. *There.* Human interest angle on what our masked heroes gave up to save us regular people. I wouldn't be able to ask him any follow-up questions, but I could still spin it into a thorough article.

I was in the process of silently congratulating myself for finally getting through my flustered embarrassment and presenting a professional front when Lightning flashed me a smile bright enough to rival his unnatural eyes.

"Well, I always have time for *meaningful* relationships,"

he drawled while letting his electric blue gaze travel up and down my disheveled figure. "Though they tend to be a bit on the short side. Why, are you offering? I do love a girl with curves."

My flush returned full-force.

Clearly, he wasn't going to give me anything other than sexual harassment and ridicule. I turned off my phone's camera and glared up at him, letting the rush of disappointment soothe some of my embarrassment. Nothing like realizing one of your favorite heroes is a complete dick to put things into perspective.

Lightning gave me another wink, seemingly unfazed by my glare, before glancing over his shoulders. "Ah, perhaps another time, eh? I'm needed elsewhere. Bye, darling."

Red smoke swept up around his taut body, consuming even his eerily shining eyes.

And then he was gone, vanished into thin air, just like on the TV clips I'd seen of him.

"Oh. My. God!"

The angry voice made me flinch and look over my shoulder. I'd completely forgotten that I wasn't alone in the shop while subjected to Lightning's penetrating gaze and less than polite comments.

Jennifer, my long-suffering barista, had climbed out from her hidey-hole. She was as disheveled as I was, after our involuntary time underneath the coffee shop's furniture, but somehow she still managed to look cute as a button. I'd envied her glowing mediterranean skin tone and big smile since my first visit to the shop.

"Did he just... did he *actually* sexually harass you?"

I grimaced, relieved I wasn't the only one who'd caught on to the true nature of our favorite "hero." But I guess if anyone would have, it'd be Jennifer. She certainly had experience with assholes making inappropriate comments while she was working.

She was exactly what men drooled over when they thought of 'curvy and petite', with round hips and perky, smallish boobs, which had caused more than one pervy customer to get thrown out of the shop. It was probably a good thing Lightning hadn't zeroed in on her—she'd have beaten him with a broom.

"I can't believe him," I seethed.

"What are you going to do about it?" she asked, eying my phone with the offensive footage. "He shouldn't get away with speaking to women like that, just because he's a superhuman."

She had a point.

And despite my disillusioned state, I wasn't about to give up my footage of the guy. Even if he wasn't the Golden Boy I'd always imagined, I could still write an article about him that would generate some traffic for my unassuming blog. A good article.

My lips pinched as I recalled Lightning's tone when he'd called me a *serious reporter*. I would show him exactly how serious I could be—as opposed to all those journalists who fawned all over him and the other vigilantes in St. Anthony.

TWO

It is entirely possible, and perhaps even plausible, that this over reliance on what is essentially glorified vigilantes is letting us become docile. We do not question why the mayor relies on these unregulated superhumans rather than put proper policing efforts in place to combat the crime running amok in our streets. We do not question the right of this self-appointed militia to dispense the punishments they see fit.

And who would? Every week there is a new story of citizens being saved by these masked heroes, and we turn a blind eye to their less than savory tactics or sexist remarks, because without them, we know we're doomed.

I *am worried.* I *am questioning this practice.*

When will the time come that our heroes won't be satisfied with a couple of rude remarks? What will the long-term price be?

And why is the mayor not lifting a finger to change what is, at its core, an easily corruptible system in place for the protection of us, the citizens of St. Anthony?

I leaned back in my chair and exhaled. This was possibly the best work I'd done since leaving college, and I was pretty damn proud of myself. Not to mention the gratification I felt for having used my resentment with Lightning's comments to fuel a serious and well thought-out article that could raise an important debate about the superhumans. And I'd used his smugness as a springboard.

It wasn't that I was in any way ungrateful for being saved from quite probably getting a face full of lead. When I thought back to lying there on the coffee shop's cold floor, staring into the barrel of that automatic weapon, goosebumps spread across my entire body. I had always known St. Anthony was a cesspit of crime and corruption, but going from reading about the violence to suddenly being part of the statistics was something else entirely.

But as thankful as I was to Lightning for saving my chubby behind, his rude comments had shaken me out of my hero worship, and that gave an entirely new perspective on the way our city relied on vigilantes to protect us against the darkness on our streets. They acted above the law by taking matters into their own hands—and were praised as heroes for it, because they saved all of us who couldn't save ourselves.

But did that make them safe to rely on? Did they believe themselves raised above us, like the demigods we treated them as? And how long before that turned dangerous? There was no way that amount of power wouldn't corrupt someone, and Lightning's arrogance might just be a sign of that.

So that was what I'd written about, to go along with the video I'd shot of him.

It wasn't a hateful article, like the ones written by people who wanted all superhumans locked away in concrete prisons deep underneath the Earth's surface, but it did raise a lot of tough questions I'd been too blind to see before my encounter with Lightning.

I got up from my desk and stretched, cringing when my back popped. I'd spent hours on that damn article, even forgetting to eat along the way, and it was now way past dinnertime.

Feeling pretty great about myself I plodded over to the kitchen section of my open plan loft apartment to rummage around in the fridge. It was the first time in a long time that I felt like I had really done something that mattered. Sure, my blog was just one, small voice, but if I could have the epiphany I'd had from Lightning's attitude, then maybe someone else watching the video and reading my article would also wake up from this daze of hero worship we found ourselves in. And then maybe we could start looking at what we had been missing while staring starry-eyed at the people doing the job the authorities were meant to.

While eating yogurt and banana slices—straight from the tub, like a lady—I considered calling Trish to brag. As a bit of a loner, Trish was the only friend from college I really kept in touch with these days, but I knew from experience that calling my friend after ten on a work night was a bad idea. Unlike me, she had gone straight into a high-profile career at the local news station, and I wasn't particularly in the mood to have my good spirit brought down by Trish telling me I knew nothing about the *"responsibilities of a real adult."*

So instead, I resigned myself to waiting to share my excitement, and instead decided to spend the rest of the night watching Netflix. For once, I felt like I'd earned a lazy night.

I WAS HALFWAY through *Paranormal Activity* 3, for the umpteenth time wondering why the heck I never learned that watching horror flicks while alone in my dark loft studio was a bad idea, when I first realized that something was wrong.

At first, I thought the creeping along my skin was simply my body reacting to the terrifying scenes unfolding on my TV. But when the sensation turned into an intense feeling of discomfort, like a prickling at the back of my neck, I finally recognized it for what it was.

Someone was watching me.

My pulse quickened instantly as if my heart was trying to escape my chest, and a sickening feeling of dread nestled in my stomach. Maybe I was just being paranoid. I lived on the fourteenth floor, and I would have heard someone trying to get in through the bolted front door. I was all alone.

Yet the feeling of being watched persisted, intensifying with each of my shallow breaths.

I was not alone.

Despite my attempt at rationalization, I knew something was very, very wrong. While being remarkably average in almost all areas of life, the one thing that I did have going for me was strong instincts—and right now, they were screaming at me about predators in the shadows of my safe haven.

Slowly, I reached for the remote and turned off the TV. Only silence met me when I strained for any signs of life to back up my sense of foreboding.

"Hello?"

I don't know why I called out into the silent room. I'd certainly watched enough horror movies to know that *that* never ended well. And what did I expect, really? A potential burglar-slash-murderer to answer me?

"Hello to you, little Kittykat," a smooth, dark voice answered from somewhere over by the kitchen.

I squeaked and scrambled off the couch, holding the remote out in front of my like a weapon as I stared wildly into the shadows. "W-who are you?"

The intruder stepped out into the soft light emanating from the only lamp I had left on in the entire apartment. He was tall and strong, the muscles in his torso and arms clearly outlined through the crimson and charcoal suit he wore. His full lips were pulled into a smirk, and behind the mask covering the upper half of his face, blue eyes shone eerily.

Lightning.

He strolled over to my computer, letting his gloved fingers dance across the desk as he took in his surroundings. Like he had all the right in the world to be in my home.

"What are you doing here?" I finally managed to say. Though my heart rate was slowing, my brain struggled with the idea of the city's favorite hero suddenly appearing in my apartment. My disillusionment with his noble character aside, I was fairly certain he wasn't here to murder me, but I still couldn't wrap my mind around why Lightning was *here,* in my home.

"You wrote an interesting article," he said, finally taking his eyes off my belongings to lock them on mine. The sensation of suddenly being rooted to the spot was unnerving, to say the least. I felt that disturbing tingle down my spine again, as if some primitive part of my body recognized his looming power. I got the errant thought that, if he wanted to, he could hurt me, and I wouldn't be able to stop him.

My heart sped up again, and I had to bite my lip hard to stop it from trembling.

"You didn't like it?" My voice sounded hoarse to my own ears, roughened by the fear I was struggling to keep at bay. He *was* one of the good guys, despite his arrogance. He didn't go around murdering innocents and corrupting the governing powers, like some of the superhumans did. Yet he had broken into my home—the one place in this city I should be safe. And I had written less than stellar things about him.

"Well, it didn't cast me in the best light," he said, the smirk slipping back into place. It looked like it belonged there, quirking his soft mouth into an expression of amused arrogance. "But you did have some interesting points, and I couldn't help but wonder where you got those ideas about the mayor and us supes from?"

I blinked, more confused than ever. "You mean... the part about Mayor Wilkins relying on vigilantes to keep the streets safe while corruption spreads in all areas of the city?"

"Yes, that part." Lightning narrowed his eyes. The smirk slid off his face, leaving a thin, grim line in its place. "I need you to give me your source, and I need it now."

"I-I don't have any sources." I didn't like the change in his demeanor. The unnerving reality of his presence in my dark apartment grew to a suffocating pressure against my frayed nerves as the power behind his gaze seemed to rush to the surface. "I just wrote the article after you..." I managed to stop myself before I added *"turned out to be a jerk."*

Lightning cocked his head, and then he walked as smoothly as a stalking panther from the desk across the open floor until he stood right in front of me. I did my best not to flinch away, but I couldn't help breathing harder as I tilted my head back to keep my eyes on him. Despite my previous assurance to myself that he was one of the good guys, being this close to his towering frame made keeping my nerves in check more than a little difficult.

"Are you telling me that you wrote an article practically accusing the mayor of corruption on a whim?"

"Um..." I hadn't fully formed that thought in my mind while writing the piece. I'd just pointed out some possible loopholes with the way things were run in St. Anthony, but it wasn't that far of a leap to make. And then it dawned on me. If Lightning was here, asking questions about my sources... My eyes widened.

"Oh, my God! He *is* corrupt! Isn't he?"

Annoyance filtered across the superhuman's features, but he remained silent as he studied me.

"Is that why you're here?" I asked. "To shut me up?" Was he *working* for the mayor? My mind was suddenly alight with conspiracy theories any of the crazy bloggers bemoaning the existence of superhumans would have been proud of. But that was just it—there were plenty of crazies out there, telling the world that the mayor was corrupt and that even the supposedly good *"supes,"* as Lightning referred to his kind, were dangerous. Why did *I* get a visit from the friendly, neighborhood hero?

Lightning scoffed, but didn't move his unnerving gaze from mine. "If you were smart, you would stay clear of antagonizing the mayor and the supe community, little girl. But if you insist, I'm not gonna stop you."

I gaped up at him. "Then why are you here? And if it's so dangerous to antagonize you and the mayor, then why is *The Truth* still allowed to publish all his ramblings?"

Lightning rolled his eyes and finally looked away, toward my dark computer screen. "I thought you were a *serious* reporter? You'd think you would know the answers to those questions. I'm here because I thought you had access to information that I need, not just random speculations. And *The Truth*," his gloved fingers actually did air quotes as he named the city's most laughed-at news blog, "never hits close to home, so it's not a threat. You, my sweet one—you did. And you are undoubtedly going to regret it."

Fear started creeping up my spine again, but this time it was not for the masked intruder. "You mean...?"

He shrugged. "It's unlikely I'm the only one who assumed you actually knew what you were writing about."

About a million different images of what that meant crowded my mind. My stomach clenched as I imagined my own mutilated corpse being fished out of the river. If Lightning was right, and some of the more unscrupulous of the superhumans decided I was a problem...

"What am I going to do?" I stared up at the masked man, completely forgetting that he wasn't necessarily the uncompromising hero everyone thought he was. "Please, you have to help me!"

Lightning pursed his lips. His eerie eyes had a distinctly sardonic slant. "Oh, I do, do I? I thought I was '*a symptom of everything that's rotten and diseased in the Dark City,*' not '*the masked hero the people of St. Anthony rely on when their elected officials fail them.*' "

Hot anger mixed with my panic. Was he really mocking me?

"I'm glad my prospective death amuses you!" I hissed, giving him my best glare. "You're even more of a scumbag than I thought." Okay, so perhaps antagonizing the unnaturally strong man who'd broken into my home wasn't the smartest choice. I grimaced and stroked a hand across my face to calm myself. "I'm sorry. I—"

"Have a big mouth and an unfortunate temper?" he interrupted. He grinned, but behind the blue light of his eyes lay something slightly sinister. "Maybe you could show me what else that wicked little tongue of yours is good at."

My cheeks warmed at his less-than-subtle insinuation, and I narrowed my eyes at him in warning. I might have been desperate for his help, and yeah, he was mouth-wateringly good-looking, even with that mask, but suggesting I get on my knees to earn his protection was clearly just to get back at me for my article. "Some hero you are."

"I never claimed to be a *hero*. Maybe I just like saving pretty girls so they'll suck my cock, and somewhere along the way, people started assuming I did it out of the goodness of my heart?"

He was toying with me. I knew it, yet his crude words and the way he was looking at me, as if I was something to be devoured, had my heart throbbing hard in my chest. Pressure seemed to wrap itself around me, caressing my skin and fogging up my mind. Uninvited images of wrapping my lips around his hard cock broke through my flustered annoyance, and something down low *clenched* in wanton sympathy. A soft groan made its way out of my throat and hung in the air between us as an audible proof of my mind and body's sudden betrayal.

I shook my head and ripped my gaze from his, trying to get a grip. What the heck was going on here? Seconds ago, I'd been terrified and more than a little annoyed with him, for pity's sake!

"What's the matter, darling?" Lightning's voice was a soft, sensual purr, and it made my nipples pebble inside my loose t-shirt. "Is there something you want?"

The image of his cock flashed in my mind's eye again, but I managed to bite my lip before I moaned. And suddenly it dawned on me. It was *him.* He was using some sort of *power* against me!

Outraged, I snapped my focus back to him. "What the hell do you think you're doing? Stop that *right now,* or I swear to God, I'll—"

The soft brush of his thumb against my bottom lip made my voice falter into a low whimper. His touch was warm, and even though it was light as a butterfly's wings, it sent a shock of electricity straight to my clit.

"Or you'll what, Kittykat?" His voice swept over me as lightly as his touch, turning my insides to liquid heat. His eyes burned into mine, pushing at something at the very core of my being.

Oh, God. Heat from his body seemed to melt into my pores as he moved closer, ruining any ability I might have possessed to resist him. I tilted my head back and parted my lips, staring up at him. He was so impossibly beautiful, every line and every angle oozing raw masculinity. And above it all those strange eyes glowed, demanding my submission.

He dipped his head down and I swayed mindlessly toward him in search of the kiss my lips were tingling with anticipation for. But instead of pressing his mouth to mine, he went for the side of my head, letting his sweltering breath tickle across my ear.

"If I was truly the asshole you made me out to be, I would bend you over the couch and fuck you rough and deep while you are high on my influence."

I shuddered as the thought of his powerful body forcing me down and spreading me open made a rush of liquid soak my panties. God, how I wanted that, wanted *him*...

Lightning brushed his lips over the side of my neck, and I tipped my head to allow him better access. While I might have been aware, on some distant level, that he was manipulating me, it felt too good to fight it.

He took the opportunity to turn me around and, before I managed to even wonder at what he was going to do, he sank his teeth into the back of my neck.

Bursts of sensation shot through my nerves and into my very blood as he clamped down on the sensitive pressure points there.

"Ooh!" I moaned, my body going limp even as my arousal spiked. My mind went as lax as my body as I surrendered completely. Yet as soon as I closed my eyes and gave in to the dark rush of endorphins, he let go.

I stumbled forward and blinked. The pressure of his powers withdrew from both my body and mind, leaving my thoughts clear as day again. Unfortunately, the uncomfortable ache between my legs didn't disappear, nor did the wet reminder of what he'd been able to do to me.

Outraged, and a little frightened, I spun back around to stare at the man who had just made my body burn with need.

Lightning smirked down at me, clearly enjoying my frazzled state. "You're welcome."

I blinked, and the fear subsided somewhat as my anger took the front seat. "I'm *welcome?* What the fuck was that! Y-you just ... *mind-raped* me!"

"That, Kittykat, was a taste of why you need to start being smarter, if you want to survive. You think someone like The Shade will stop when I did? You think making your pussy tingle is anywhere close to what some of the bad supes would do to you? When you wrote that article, you stepped into my world—and it's a dangerous place for a human."

I couldn't hold back the cold shiver that traveled up my spine when he named the scariest villain this city had ever known. "T-The Shade? You really think that he would come for me?"

Lightning shrugged. "I wouldn't be too surprised. He's not your biggest concern, though. Not anymore. My mark on your neck should warn the other supes off—even that bastard. Keep your head down and write about what you normally do—flowers or dresses, or whatever. Hopefully, that should be enough to get you off the radar again."

I touched the back of my neck where my skin still throbbed from his bite. There were far too many *"shoulds"* and *"hopefullys"* in Lightning's reassurance for my liking, but he seemed calm enough about it to soothe some of my worries.

I forced my fingers away from my nape. "So... I'm safe?"

Lightning shook his head as if I was a particularly slow child before finally turning away from me and walking back toward the kitchen. "No, Kathryn. You're not safe. You will never be *safe* in this city. But if you start acting smart, you have a chance. Don't stick your nose where it doesn't belong —my mark won't protect you if you overstep again."

"What does it mean? Your mark?" I asked as I took a few

hesitant steps after him. "Why does it warn the other super-humans away?"

His low chuckle emanated from the darkened kitchen. When I got close enough, I saw his shaded outline crouched on my open window ledge, ready to leap out into the night. He turned his face toward me, and his blue gaze lit up his wry smile.

"It means you're mine, Kittykat."

THREE

As it turned out, I had been right when I thought a video of Lightning would boost my blog traffic. I found this out after I logged on to delete my article, but by that point, it was already way too late. It was all over the Internet, alongside my stupidly smiling profile picture. Maybe if I'd had the wits to take it down immediately after Lightning's surprise visit, I would have had a chance, but I'd been way too shell-shocked to be that smart.

I'd spent the entire night in a fitful daze, tossing and turning in my bed—lost between terrifying nightmares of being chased by everything evil in St. Anthony and surges of inexplicable lust. Even now, when I was sitting bleary-eyed from lack of sleep, sipping my coffee and staring at my face next to *The Truth's* coverage of my article, I squirmed in my seat when I thought about my late-night guest.

You're mine, he'd said.

What the heck was *that* supposed to mean? Did super-humans own us regulars like livestock? Would someone killing me be viewed like cattle theft used to be viewed in the old west? It had been abundantly clear last night that I didn't know anything about the true nature of the people with special abilities who walked among us, and right now, that thought worried me more than it ever had.

Frankly, it terrified me.

The way Lightning had manipulated either my mind or body—I wasn't entirely sure which—had some pretty horrible implications. If they could mind-fuck with everybody, then they could control *everything,* and no one would be the wiser. Was that what this whole thing was about? Was the mayor being corrupted by the bad superhumans via mind control?

My pussy throbbed longingly at the thought of Lightning's hot breath against my ear, whispering about the filthy things he could have done to me while my will was his to control.

"For fuck's sake," I hissed, willing my body to stop behaving like it belonged to a cat in heat. Lightning had been the poster boy for sexist pricks everywhere last night, and there was absolutely no need for my ovaries to spazz out like this a full ten hours after he'd released me from the mind control, or whatever it was.

It disturbed me. Especially because some small part of me still wished he would have followed through with his threats of bending me over the sofa and having his way with me.

At that particularly thought, I decided it was time for a shower. Preferably a cold one. And after, when my body was hopefully done committing mutiny, I could try to figure out the mess my article had left me in.

I DIDN'T GET a chance to sit down and decide how I could best go about following Lightning's advice, because just as I was toweling off my hair, Trish called.

"*Kat!*" she bellowed when I picked up. I cringed and tried to suppress the memory of the way Lightning had called me *Kittykat*.

"Hi, Trish. What's up?"

"What's up? Oh, only that my bestie nailed an interview with the city's hottest commodity! You're a rock star, Kathryn! Congratulations."

I smiled wryly as I made my way to the kitchen on bare feet. My loft studio was high off the ground, and with the closest high rise of equal height to my building being far enough away that I could walk around naked without anyone seeing me through the windows that lined the entire outer wall. Unless they used their superhuman powers to scale the building and climb in my kitchen window. I gave said window an annoyed frown.

"Thanks. It's not that big a deal, though. He wasn't exactly the best interviewee. Did you see it? He was such an ass."

She laughed into the phone. "He could have been reciting the movements of the stock market and people would have gobbled up every second of it. And your article? Wow! Didn't know you had it in you, Kat! Will you be following up with the mayor's office for a quote? You could really use this to launch your career, if you work it right."

I huffed. Yeah, I could have—if doing so wouldn't end with me floating downriver. It was so infuriating to know I had a hold of the end of the long, tangled thread that could lead me into the heart of St. Anthony's corruption, yet if I followed it, I would die. Once again, the criminals feeding off the city's population had won.

Trish seemed to pick up on my hesitation.

"Is something wrong, Kat?"

I paused, biting my lip as I contemplated whether or not to tell her about my late-night visitor. I was pretty sure doing so wouldn't be what Lightning would class as *smart,* but I could really use some level-headed input about this whole mess before my head exploded.

"Kat?" she prompted when my silent debate with myself had apparently gone on for long enough. "What happened?"

She sounded exactly like she had the time in college I'd bombed a test and she'd had to talk me down from drowning my sorrows in a pitcher of stale beer. The memory made my unease settle somewhat. This was Trish—my best friend, and even if life had moved in different directions for us, I could still trust her to talk me through this.

"Lightning came by my apartment last night."

"What?!" Her shriek pierced my skull and I held the phone out from my ear. "Oh my God, Kat. Oh my God! What was he like? What did he want?"

I suppose I couldn't really blame her for the excitement, but I found it pretty hard to align the elation in her voice with the events of the prior night.

"He wanted me to give up my source for that article. Only I didn't have one. I just posted a lot of what-ifs, questions, and... I think I'm in some serious trouble, Trish."

As I told my friend what had happened—leaving out the disturbing part where I'd been about ready to throw myself at Lightning and ravish him, and the way he'd bitten me to mark me as *his*—she grew silent on the other end of the line. When I was finally done, she heaved a sigh into the phone.

"Fuck."

I couldn't really argue there.

"I don't know what to do," I admitted. "I *think* he meant that he would try to protect me, but I'm still sufficiently terrified that if I had the money I might leave the city today. And—"

"And you want to investigate this further, don't you?"

"Yeah." I opened the fridge to look for something to eat. Preferably something covered in chocolate. I'd always been a stress-eater, which my softer-than-average figure bore testament to. "I know, it's crazy, and I'm not going to, but..."

"But a lead like this is every reporter's wet dream. Even if they are a blogging reporter," Trish finished when I trailed off.

I ignored the comment about my chosen career path—if you could even call it that—and pulled a peanut butter and jelly sandwich I'd made the day before out of the fridge. "I guess. But Lightning was pretty damn clear—if I keep writing about this, I'm..." I didn't have the stomach to say *dead*.

"What if you didn't write about it?"

I frowned at my sandwich. "I wasn't planning to."

My friend sighed again. "What I meant was—what if you didn't write about it *yet,* but gathered more evidence quietly? Once you have something that will stick, you come to me. My network knows how to protect its journalists, and for a story as big as this could get—they would extend it to a freelancer I worked with, too."

The "I worked with" part didn't escape my attention, and I had to bite back a snarky retort. Trish was brilliant, but she did have a tendency to get kind of pushy about claiming credit for work we'd both contributed to back in college. But this wasn't college. This was so much more serious, and her idea did sound good. Maybe I could help dig out some of the corruption in St. Anthony without risking my life. The thought of what this could do for my career, even if I did share credit with Trish, admittedly also stirred at the back of my mind.

"I'll think about it."

FOUR

The problem with gathering evidence about anything involving the superhumans, whether quietly or otherwise, was that there was nowhere to go for actual facts. Everything that had ever been written about them was largely speculation, and the scant photos and videos featuring any of them didn't give much away, apart from proving beyond a doubt that they certainly were more than human.

Which meant that my quiet investigation came to an abrupt halt before it ever really began.

The truth was that as long as Lightning didn't climb in my window and offer up anything, I had no chance of unveiling whatever it was I'd stumbled across.

I sighed as I clicked through image after image on Google for the third day, without having any clue how to proceed with my research. Many of the pictures were of Lightning, and I had the unkind thought that he possibly enjoyed being on the front cover of magazines more than your average vigilante.

He did look good in all of them, though. Tall, lean, and

carved from rock, with every single muscle in his torso and legs clearly defined through his trademark suit. I stared at a picture of him standing in front of a fiery background, smiling. I remembered when it had been taken just over a month ago. He and Red Rider—the hero who dressed in all red and generally stayed in the south end of the city—had saved several people from a burning building. He seemed as composed in that picture as he had while I'd attempted to interview him. There was no hint of the darker side—the side I'd experienced as he swathed my mind in lust.

A shiver traveled through my body and ended with a zing in my clit. I groaned and clamped my thighs together in an effort to resist the urge to touch myself.

Goddamn that man! Since he had messed with my mind, I'd found it very hard to concentrate without getting the need to go find my vibrator. In the beginning I had been worried that some element of his mind control was still lingering, but as the days progressed, it became painfully clear that it was more of a Pavlovian response from my traitorous body. Whenever I spent too much time looking at pictures of the masked hero, or thinking about the way his teeth had felt against my nape, my pussy would ache with need, as if yearning for it bad enough would make his cock materialize inside of me.

The fact that Lightning's obscene display was the closest I'd been to actual sex in a very long time probably didn't help matters, either. Looking for a boyfriend when you were a chubby introvert in a city obsessed with all things superficial was not exactly easy.

Lightning hadn't seemed the least bit concerned about my not-exactly-model-sized body, though. Quite the opposite, if his remark about liking "curvy women" was anything to go by. Of course, he might have just been full of shit and looking to manipulate me. He certainly hadn't stayed behind to finish the job after he'd released me from the mind control.

I rubbed at the back of my neck where he had bitten me. The skin there tingled in a way that made my nipples hard, as if the ghost of his mouth brushed against it every time I thought about how it had felt to be so completely under a man's control. Great. Even though my original fascination with Lightning had been quelled by his sexist attitude, it would seem that my hormones had no problem reducing me to a drooling idiot.

Some *serious reporter* I was. Taken out of the game by my own ovaries and a fear of being found out before I'd even done anything noteworthy. Trish would have uncovered something useful by now, if she was the frontrunner for this story. Heck, any *real* reporter probably would have.

I huffed at that particular thought. As much as I loved the relaxed atmosphere of being a small-time blogger, I couldn't deny that thread of envy lurking somewhere in the shameful depths of my subconscious. Trish had always been better than me in college, more driven, so it was no wonder her career was so much more high-powered than mine. There was still just that sliver of me that wished I could prove to myself that I was as capable a reporter as she was, just once.

It was probably that sliver that made me get up from my desk, grab my purse, and head out the door before my cautious side could kick in.

I SHOULD HAVE PLANNED my field trip better.

Heck, planning it at all would have been a step up from my rash decision to do something, anything.

The murky streets of St. Anthony's industrial quarter were dimming even more as the sun set behind the old brick buildings. My pulse was throbbing in my throat when darkness descended around me, leaving only the lights from the skyline to illuminate my path.

No one lived here, and most of the buildings had been closed down during the last gang war, the companies opting to find less crime-plagued cities to operate their business from, which meant I found myself in an odd quietude. I was so used to the general noise of the city twenty-four-seven that the relative silence now felt disconcerting. I could hear my own footsteps and the sound of glass breaking underneath my shoes.

I muttered a curse under my breath and pulled out my phone so I could use the light from the display to see where I was going. I'd chosen the industrial quarter for my impromptu excursion because it was where the first incidents of a supernatural serial killer had taken place back in the Sixties. I didn't know what I was looking for exactly, but it was the best place I could think to search for any sort of clue. Or at least feel like I was doing *something,* other than drooling over pictures of Lightning.

While researching online, I'd come across a few references to the industrial quarter being the turf of a superhuman who had skinned his victims alive, and how he was the reason the first heroes had put on masks to help fight the crime our police couldn't handle. He had reigned for three years before the other superhumans killed him, which had also happened somewhere in the industrial quarter.

It wasn't that I expected to trip over his hidden lair—the

police had scoured the area before and after his death without any luck—but maybe I could find... well, anything that could point me in the direction of modern day's supernatural crime.

Of course, looking around in the daytime would have probably made things a lot easier, I realized as I peered up at the dark storehouses. Using my phone to illuminate them ruined my night vision, so I put it back in my bag and tried to calm the anxiety stirring in my gut.

No one was here, not even gangs anymore, as there was nothing left to steal. All the warehouses had been stripped of any valuables, and so even most criminals stayed away. Still, my instincts kept muttering louder and louder about all the things that could lurk in the dark corners as I slowly made my way through the dirty streets, stepping over broken glass and fallen bricks for every other step.

I kept glancing over my shoulder, but saw nothing but darkness behind me. It was the same eerie sense of being watched as I'd felt in my apartment, but this time, I didn't call out. Instead, when the nagging sensation grew so strong I could no longer ignore it, I finally decided that it was high time I started making my way back home. While the excursion had been a complete waste of time, I didn't want to push my luck.

Lightning's promised protection had been what made me brave the secluded industrial quarter in the first place, but if the sensation of being watched wasn't just my nerves getting the better of me, then I really didn't want to test how effective his mark was.

I turned around to start heading back, intent on making it home before the night-time TV programming started and maybe calming down my hyper-alert nerves with a mug of hot chocolate. That was when I saw something moving in the shadows some twenty yards away.

Tendrils of instant and overwhelming fear made my entire body freeze up. I should have started running then and there, but I didn't—I couldn't. My mind was now flooded by the torrent of impressions my panicked sixth sense had been trying to get through before.

I could hear footsteps now, moving closer and closer, quiet whispers and the occasional crunch of glass underneath heavy boots. How long had they been stalking me? And *why?* It had been three days since the article—three days of absolutely no indication that anyone other than Lightning had as much as raised an eyebrow at my blog. Not to mention that no one could have the faintest idea what I was looking for here—heck, *I* didn't know what I was looking for.

"Lightning? I know you're following me."

My own trembling voice echoed off the deserted buildings. Somewhere deep down I knew it wasn't Lightning, but oh, how I hoped it was.

There was no reply from the shadowed road behind me, and no more movement, either. The silence made my spine itch. Slowly, I took a step backwards.

"Lightning?" I whispered.

Something shifted just at the edge of my field of vision, and I snapped my head to the left just in time to see a figure peel away from the shadows behind an old dumpster. A man, I could tell as he walked closer. Faint light from the city reflected off the knife he held in his left hand. Then other shadowy figures emerged from the darkness, joining the first. Four more men, all carrying some form of weapons, as far as I could tell.

My heart slammed into my ribs as I stared at them. Then I did the first smart thing I'd done all night.

I turned around and ran.

I've never been much of a runner, but when I heard my stalkers giving chase, my feet seemed to fly across the uneven tarmac. I stumbled over the broken bricks and garbage left in the gutters, yet kept moving forward and away from what I knew would be my end.

"There's nowhere to run," a snarl sounded behind me, much closer than it should have been. "Nowhere to hide."

Oh, God! The sound of his voice was even worse than their previous silence had been, somehow hammering home their intent. Their intent to cause me harm. My adrenaline, already pumping wildly through my bloodstream, spiked higher, and I pushed my legs to move faster. *Away!* I needed to get away from these men, whoever they were.

My panicked thoughts came to an abrupt halt when I looked up and saw the path ahead of me blocked off by a tall, chain-link fence crowned with barbed wire. I didn't pause to consider my options before I threw myself down the narrow alleyway opening up to the left, my only option for escaping.

But about thirty yards later, my flight ended.

I skidded to a stop in front of the brick wall blocking off the passageway, my eyes desperately searching for a way out. There was none. I was trapped.

No, no, no! I could taste bile on my tongue as I whipped around to see my pursuers slowing to a walk after rounding the corner to the alleyway.

"Well, well," one of them —the leader, I think—purred as he stopped less than six feet from me, flanked by two of the other men.

"What do we have here? A nosy little reporter bitch out

on her own in the most deserted place in the damn city? Odd behavior, isn't it, boys?"

I swallowed and pressed my back up against the wall, wishing I could just melt into it. If they knew I was a reporter, then they weren't just random thugs out to terrorize idiotic women meandering around abandoned warehouses on their own. They were here specifically for me—for what they thought I knew.

Even though their eyes weren't glowing, marking them as superhumans, my hands flew to the back of my neck to push my braid away so I could display the place Lightning had bitten me. There was nothing to see with my human eyesight, though I had looked in the mirror more than once, but the way the skin tingled every time I touched it, there was clearly some sort of magic infused there. Hopefully, these men would know what it meant.

"I'm his! I'm Lightning's, so back off!" I shouted. Even without the shaky note of hysteria in my voice, the words themselves sounded a lot more ridiculous than they had in my head.

"Lightning," the man on the right spat, brandishing what looked like a crowbar. It made a horrible screeching noise as he scraped it against the wall beside him. "No one gives a shit about you, cunt, least of all some high and mighty *supe.* But maybe if you spread your legs for us before we take you back to the boss, we'll go easier on you when he asks us to get whatever information he wants from you. What do you say? Wanna keep your fingers?"

Nausea exploded in my stomach. They were going to rape and mutilate me for information I didn't have, and as I stared into the cold eyes of my attackers, I had no delusions that I was going to live afterward.

"*Help!* Help me!"

The piercing scream ripping from my throat seemed to throw the men into motion.

It felt as if I was seeing the world through a blur as the men crashed against me, grabbing for my wrists and neck. I fought them on pure instinct, clawing and kicking and biting like a wild animal, but it was useless against their brute force.

A stinging slap smacked my head into the wall, dazing me for a moment, and when I regained my focus, my wrists had been zip tied together and a strong hand had a hold of my jaw, pressing hard enough to make tears spring to my eyes. I tried kneeing the man who was keeping my body pressed against the wall in the groin, but all I got out of that was a hard punch to my stomach.

Pain exploded in crippling waves. I slumped to the floor, dry heaving from agony unlike anything I'd experienced since the time I broke my leg after falling out of a tree house in second grade. I'd never been one to get into fights, and this was the first time someone had ever truly punched me. Actually experiencing the sort of pain I'd feared from them left me stunned and gasping for air.

"Well, you're fucked now," someone growled above me. "Think you can kick me in the balls, huh? I'll fucking show you!"

I cried out when a heavy boot impacted with my thighs, kicking them apart, and again when someone grabbed my pants and ripped, leaving my lower body exposed to the cool air.

"Guess we'll fuck your pussy *and* cut off your fingers. And maybe your toes too, just for the hell of it."

Whatever hadn't kicked in of my survival instincts before did so now. I scrambled on the ground to get up and run, not caring that I was bound or that the five men in the alley with me were much stronger and undoubtedly also faster than me. All that mattered was getting away.

Snide laughter echoed through the alleyway as the men watched me crawl a few feet before one of them placed a foot on my back and stepped down, landing me flat on my stomach with a pained cry.

"Where do you think you're going, cunt? We're just about to get star—"

The voice was interrupted by a soft thud and an odd, metallic singing through the air directly above me, followed by a gurgle from the man who had been taunting me.

Then another, much louder thud echoed through the alley as his big body collapsed next to me. I stared into his face that was still locked in frozen surprise. A trickle of blood dripped from the corner of his mouth. He was dead.

Before I managed another scream, the alleyway exploded into movement and shouts that quickly turned into howls of pain.

As quickly as I could, I turned over onto my back to see what the heck was going on. The sight that met my eyes sent pure terror through my body.

The Shade.

His name pounded in my head as the large shadow that had joined us in the alley whirled around, slicing through my attackers with his iconic dual blades. Blood and chunks of body parts rained around me like macabre confetti at a parade. In what was probably less than ten seconds, though it felt like an eternity, only one of the thugs was left standing, and he was too preoccupied with clutching at his bleeding arm stump to put up any resistance. With an almost casual flick of his wrist, The Shade swung one sword, decapitating him.

I was vaguely aware of my entire body trembling like a leaf, but the vast majority of my focus was glued to the dark figure.

He looked down for a moment, surveying his handiwork before pushing at one of the bodies with his foot, as if testing if his victim was truly dead.

And then his glowing blue gaze met mine.

I wanted to scream, or to scramble away, but my body was too numb to do either. I could do nothing but watch as The Shade pointed the tip of one blade at my throat, letting the flat side nudge my chin up.

"So," he said, his voice a low hum in the silence, "you belong to Lightning?"

FIVE

There were bad men in this city. Some preyed on the weak and helpless. Some terrorized entire neighborhoods, profiting off the despair festering in St. Anthony's very core.

None of them were more than ripples in the darkness compared to The Shade.

He was the quintessential Evil, having slaughtered thousands for no other reason than his own amusement, if the rumors were to be believed, and he possessed no such thing as a conscience. Or a soul. And he was here, alone in the alley. With me.

The cold steel of his sword pressed just a tad firmer against my skin, and I swallowed thickly from the silent threat. Now was not the time to lose my ability to speak, if I wanted any chance at not ending up like my attackers.

"Y-yes," I croaked. "He m-marked me."

"He did, did he? And yet here you are, wandering around in the darkness without any protection. How... curious. Get up." The last two words were an unmistakable command, though his voice remained eerily soft.

I scrambled to obey, using my bound arms to prop my body up against the wall. The Shade watched me as I somehow managed to get my abused body upright, keeping his sword pointed at my throat until I was finally on my feet.

"And how come Lightning's favored pet is traipsing around the industrial quarter late at night? I would have thought even he would consider that a terrible idea. He knows what lurks in the darkness in this city."

The way he spat out Lightning's name, as if it tasted disgusting on his tongue, made me remember the rumored rivalry between the two superhumans. Apparently there was something to it—I could just hope that Lightning had been right when he said that even The Shade wouldn't harm me as long as I carried his mark, despite whatever animosity hung between them.

"He doesn't know," I said, feeling just a touch of relief when he finally lowered his sword. Not that he needed it to harm me.

"Oh?" His full lips curled into a wry smile. "The little kitten is sneaking around behind her master's back? What could possibly draw that sort of disobedience out of a soft, little human?"

Master? Disobedience? I frowned at the implication. "He's not my *master*."

I probably should have kept my mouth shut. In fact, when I saw the dangerous shift in The Shade's glowing eyes, I knew I should have. I instinctively pressed my back against the wall behind me, wishing that he would stop staring at me like I was a particularly tasty-looking mouse and he was a cat.

"If he took you as his, you would not think to question the terminology." The Shade lifted one sword again, his perfectly-defined muscles flexing behind the skin-tight black suit. "Show me your mark."

Dread mixed with the fear pulsing through my veins in steady beats. I had zero desire to turn my head and display my vulnerable neck to this dark creature, but I only had to glance at the floor to get the gist of what would likely happen if I disobeyed him. Even the relative darkness of the alleyway couldn't completely hide the bloody display.

Slowly, I turned my head and pushed my braid out of the way, trying to keep my eyes on The Shade as his focus flickered from my face to my exposed neck.

Yet despite my attempt at following his movements, the gust of wind enveloping me was the only warning I had before he was suddenly standing less than six inches from me, his big frame looming over me. He was *huge*. I hadn't realized just how massive he really was before, because his lithe movements as he unleashed death on my attackers were a complete contrast to the bulk of his body, but now... now, that he was so close he was blocking off my view of the skyline with his body, I noticed that he was even bigger than Lightning.

The effect was more than a little intimidating.

I swallowed a whimper and forced myself to stand completely still when The Shade braced a hand on the wall next to me and bent his head to my neck. When he inhaled deeply just above the place Lightning had bitten me, every hair on my body stood on end. Yet it was nothing compared to how the low growl he breathed into my ear set my entire skin ablaze with fear and... and something else. Something that made the goosebumps crawling along my skin harden my nipples and my breath catch in my throat.

Then he pulled back, once again towering over me.

"It would appear you haven't been fully claimed, kitten." The Shade's deep voice was hardly more than a whisper in the darkness above me, but it carried a harsher note to it now. "He forgot to fuck you."

"W-what?" I did my best to steady my breathing. Every cell in my body seemed to recognize the danger The Shade posed, and the continual supply of adrenaline was sharpening my senses beyond their normal reach, making me able to feel his body's heat and see the full curve of his mouth and a thin scar running across his upper lip in the dark. But it was also making me feel drugged, as if I didn't have a full connection from my brain to my limbs, and my legs and arms seemed oddly numb and tingly at the same time.

"You don't belong to him until you spread your legs and accept him into your soft little body." He lifted his chin to indicate the still-exposed part of my neck where I'd been bitten. Then he took a few steps back and, before I even registered the movement, sliced one razor sharp sword through the air, cutting through the zip tie around my wrists.

At my startled gasp, he lifted both arms, sliding his twin swords into the scabbards mounted on his back. I couldn't help but notice the way his muscles flexed and bulged with the movement, underlining his strength with casual ease.

"Oh," I gulped, not entirely sure what to think about any of it. The memory of how willing I had been to spread my legs for Lightning when he bit me made blood heat up my cheeks. If The Shade was speaking the truth—which, frankly, wasn't exactly a guarantee—then why had Lightning stopped when he did?

"Isn't that just typical your beloved *hero?*" The Shade took a few steps forward, once more boxing me in against the wall. Despite my newly-gained freedom, his hulking presence made me feel even more trapped than when my hands had been tied.

"He loves to be seen as the great savior, yet when push comes to shove, he doesn't have the balls to go through with it. Do you even realize how vulnerable you are out here, with a half-mark on that delicate little neck? If someone were to snap it, it would be viewed as nothing more than an insult—no laws would be broken. No, he's just arrogant enough to think the threat of his retribution is enough to warn us off."

I didn't bother mentioning that quite a few laws would be broken by killing me. A man who could slaughter five people without a moment's hesitation was clearly not referring to human law.

"P-please, don't," I managed to croak out as a full body quiver made me tremble and press harder against the wall.

He cocked his head. "Don't what? Snap your neck? You write conspiracy theories involving the supe community and the most corrupt mayor in this damned city's history, and then spend your evenings snooping around where you don't belong. One really couldn't be faulted for thinking you had a death wish, *Kathryn*."

Kathryn. He knew who I was. He knew about the fucking article.

A fresh wave of dread made me swallow in an attempt to press my heart down from my throat.

"I..."

"What are you looking for in the industrial quarter?" His entire demeanor shifted in the blink of an eye, his wide shoulders squaring up to take up even more of my field of vision. What was visible of his face for the black mask smoothed into cool stone.

"Nothing," I whispered, and then yelped when his right hand slapped against the bricks right next to my face.

The Shade leaned down, holding his face an inch from mine. He narrowed his eyes, leaving absolutely no doubt in my mind what would happen if I defied him. "Lie to me again. I dare you."

"Superhumans!" I squeaked. "I-I'm looking for supes. Or anything related to them—you."

He pulled back an inch, giving me just a bit more room to breathe. "Why?"

"I need something tangible—proof. I know my article hit on something real, and I need to find the connection so I can out the responsible parties." Outright stating that I was trying to pull down the corruption in the city to one of the worst criminals in it was surely not the smartest thing to do, but the blue gaze spearing mine gave me absolutely zero desire to test him with another lie.

The Shade smirked. "And Lightning knows nothing of this?"

"He told me to keep my head down and stay away from it," I whispered, praying my honesty would save my life.

The Shade looked downright amused, and the threatening pressure of his presence eased as he straightened back up and gave me a thoughtful look. "So you *are* a defiant little human, hm?"

"I thought you said his claim wasn't valid. If I'm not truly his, I'm not really defying him."

Now he grinned, letting the faint light from the city reflect off his white teeth. "And lippy, too. Either you're very brave, kitten, or very stupid."

At this point, I was pretty sure it was stupid.

"Even if Lightning had claimed you fully, his mark

wouldn't have protected you from human thugs. Did you really think the supe community were the only ones keeping an eye on you after that bomb you dropped on the Internet?"

"I... didn't think about it," I admitted. Shame made me bite my lip and drop my gaze. When my eyes met the dead stare of the last survivor's decapitated head I looked back up, fighting the sudden onset of nausea. Even though Lightning's visit had made me come to terms with the very real danger looking into the supes posed, I hadn't imagined it could result in humans stalking me like this.

"You're way out of your depth, little girl," The Shade said. "I don't even think you realize how far yet."

A high-pitched laugh burst past my lips before I managed to clamp my jaw shut around it.

"I think I have a pretty good idea!" I made a vague gesture toward the broken bodies on the ground, without making the mistake of looking down again. "God, I can't even think about what they would have done to me if you hadn't saved..." My voice trailed off as I realized what I was saying. Another giggle escaped my throat. "*You* saved me." The Shade had saved me from torture and death. I was so far out of my depth that I'd taken a left turn into the outright absurd.

He watched while my hysteria slowly subsided. When I finally got a hold of myself again, a wave of gratitude so strong it nearly knocked my legs out from underneath me swept through my limbs.

"Thank you. Thank you so much. If you hadn't come..."

"You would be dead," he said, his voice as soft and emotionless as when he had first spoken to me.

"If there is anything I can do to pay you back..." I grabbed for my bag on some ridiculous instinct, then realized

I must have dropped it at some point during the fight. "I've lost my bag, but if you help me find it, I can pay you..." My voice died at the incredulous look in his burning blue eyes.

"You think I killed them for money? That I am some pathetic vigilante saving damsels in distress to get paid?"

"No. I know who you are." And *what* he was. I swallowed nervously at the way his eyes flickered when he looked me over. "Why *did* you save me?"

The Shade pursed his lips and folded his arms across his chest, making his pectorals and biceps strain underneath his suit. "There is something you can do to pay me back for saving your life, Kathryn."

Uh oh. There was a quiet, but distinct foreboding behind his dismissal of my question. I looked up at him, willing my body to stop its trembling as I waited for the price he would claim in return for my life. Why hadn't I just kept my mouth shut?

"Accept my mark."

SIX

I blinked. Twice. "W-what?"

He narrowed his eyes, and the glow from them illuminated his mouth's firm set. "You heard me. Is your life worth that much, kitten?"

I wasn't entirely sure if he was threatening me with what would happen if I didn't accept. I didn't feel like asking.

"Um..." My mind raced as I stared up at him, and I wished it would stop circling back to what he'd said Lightning had failed to do to mark me properly.

"Wouldn't... Wouldn't Lightning mind? H-he said I was his." I was grasping at straws, throwing the hero's name in front of me like a flimsy shield, even though I didn't hold much hope for its effectiveness.

The Shade twisted his mouth into a dark smile, and then he leaned forward, bracing both hands on each side of my head, boxing me in fully. "Oh, I'm counting on it."

I gulped. He was way, way too close again, the heat from him radiating into my skin through my clothes.

"Look at it this way—where was he tonight? Where was

he while you were being threatened and abused? You are not safe with him as a protector. I, on the other hand, will watch over you—make sure you are safe from harm." The Shade lifted one gloved hand and let his fingers trail up my neck before he grasped my jaw. "Be smart, kitten."

Be smart. The irony of hearing Lightning's words echoed from The Shade's deviant lips wasn't lost on me.

"Now? *Here?*" I croaked, trying to think of anything that could give me just a few moments to think—to reel my mind in from his hypnotic stare and overpowering presence.

"Yes," he murmured, smiling at my lips' trembling and the undoubtedly terrified expression plastered across my face. "Now. Here. I want you to spread your legs and accept my claim."

Well, that cleared up any confusion about whether or not he intended to make up for the part Lightning had been enough of a gentleman to skip.

"I... uh, I... don't think...." My voice trailed off to an indistinguishable mumble when his burning gaze lowered to my mouth and he brushed his thumb over my lower lip. Unexpected heat traveled through me at the light touch and I recoiled as far as the wall against my back would let me.

"What are you doing?" My voice was sharp with accusation, even though my heart pounded with fear. Would he really mind-rape me into allowing this, into allowing him to... Oh, God, why was I even asking—he was The freaking Shade! Of course he would!

The Shade smiled. "I'm not doing anything, kitten. That sweet pulse between your legs is all you."

My face went burning hot the second I realized what he was talking about—my pussy was throbbing in tune with my racing heart, sending tendrils of warmth up through my abdomen. It had just been lost in the adrenaline and fear until I focused on it.

"You're making me want you," I whispered as I stared at him. "This is no better than rape."

Despite the accusation, he simply chuckled, letting his intoxicating breath sweep across my mouth. And then he dipped his head after my lips.

I didn't even realize that he'd paused just shy of connecting before I leaned into the kiss, as if drawn by a magnet.

The press of his full, soft mouth against mine made me open my eyes wide in shock. Yes, *I* had closed the final distance, lured in by that hot throb that seemed to spread and grow the longer his lips danced over mine.

"*Mmph!*" I protested, finally raising my hands from where they'd hung limply by my sides to push against his shoulders.

The Shade drew back a few inches. The heat in his eyes made me gasp, the warmth in my abdomen turning molten in response. Slowly, deliberately, he removed his black leather gloves and let them fall to the dirty ground, never breaking eye contact.

"W-we can't do this!" I stammered, despite the wanton *clenching* from down low. Oh, holy fuck, what was happening to me? I was still terrified of the man looking down at me, but my body was yielding to his softest touch. It had to be some of that mind voodoo Lightning had also pushed at me, *had* to be... though no matter how desperately I searched my mind for the same sensation of *power* enveloping my will, I found nothing.

"No? Give me one good reason." The Shade's voice was darker, huskier, and it went straight to my traitorous lower parts. My half-torn panties had actually started to feel damp. *Oh, God.*

"A reason?" I panted. Under less strenuous circumstances, I would undoubtedly have been able to come up with about a thousand reasons, starting with the fact that he was the living embodiment of evil. Right now, however, my brain was struggling to come up with anything. I ripped my gaze from his in an attempt at aiding its efforts, and my eyes fell on a dismembered hand on the ground. The resulting shudder was from anything but arousal.

"I c-can see them. The blood and..."

The Shade rolled his eyes, but before I could contemplate the weirdly human gesture, he'd grabbed me by the shoulders and spun me around so I was facing the brick wall.

"There," he hummed into my ear. The light pressure of his hand trailed down my back, slipping around my hip to my front before it reached my ruined pants. And then his fingers pressed in at just the right place, settling firmly on my clit through what was left of the fabric covering my crotch.

I jolted at the contact, straightening my back, but when I tried to shy away I was caught by the strong arm he wrapped around my waist and his decadent lips capturing my earlobe.

"Shh, give in to it. No one's here but you and me—let me take care of you. I can make all your fears go away." The Shade's hypnotic whisper was accompanied by the fingers on my clit starting to slowly draw circles against my sensitive nub, never easing the pressure.

I wasn't sure if it was his words or the throbbing need building between my legs for each stroke of his damned fingers over my swollen clit, or perhaps my mind finally giving in to the constant bombardment of fear and adrenaline, but I spread my legs for him. God help me, I spread my legs, and I invited him in.

"Good girl."

I whimpered and dug my fingers into the uneven bricks in front of me as his ministrations between my legs intensified. Fighting, and slowly losing, the battle to stay in control of my body, I told myself I had to do this. *Had to*, even though I shouldn't—

"*Ohh!*" I clamped my teeth shut, but only after the traitorous moan had interrupted my desperate attempt at justifying why I was allowing The Shade's touch. My mind was fumbling for a reason I could accept—anything that didn't involve the sweet way my pussy ached for the dangerous criminal—but came up short. Even in the depths of my despair as I clung to the wall while The Shade's thick fingers found their way into my panties and parted my soft flesh, I knew he wasn't forcing me.

The feel of warm skin against my sensitive nub made me shudder and moan again. Sharp spikes of sensation shot down my thighs and up my spine, and I bucked my hips to ease the friction. The Shade pushed his hips forward in response, pressing my body up against the bricks so I couldn't escape. He was everywhere behind me, covering every inch of my back and thighs. His hot breath teased my ear and the side of my neck, and something large and hard pressed against my lower back, reminding me of what was ahead.

"Oh, God," I whimpered, too overwhelmed by his presence to voice a protest when he resumed his firm movements against my exposed clit. I writhed uselessly in his grip, but there was nowhere to go.

Slowly, my pussy submitted to the stimulation. The too-intense zings turned to hot thrills of pleasure, and I felt my hips begin to move with the rhythm. When The Shade shifted his grip down there, slipping two fingers down through my soaked folds to my entrance, I was ready for it.

The Shade gave me no quarter—his thick fingers pushed in in one fluid movement, opening my slick pussy wider than I had been prepared for.

I mewled in protest at the unexpected stretch, but it didn't hurt—I was way too wet for his fingers to cause me pain. I didn't get a chance to process the sudden sensation of being filled before his fingers hooked, digging into my G-spot, and his teeth clamped down around the back of my neck.

Everything went white for three long seconds as I cried out at the unexpected burst of ecstasy. My hips jerked and my pussy clutched at his fingers, clamping down when he began rubbing that delicious spot rough and hard. Along with the sharp sting of his bite, it was enough to bring me to the brink of orgasm and over.

I screamed into the darkness surrounding us and scraped at the wall before my mind had even fully comprehended what was happening to my body. The rush of pleasure exploded up from my spasming pussy and hit my brain in a burst of endorphins.

Everything was blissful—peaceful.

Only when he eased the pressure against the fleshy spot inside of me did I slowly find my bearings.

I struggled to keep my footing now that I was no longer being propped up by The Shade. Then my senses returned in an unpleasantly sharp flare.

Oh, my God!! The Shade! I had just come all over The Shade's fingers, screaming like a madwoman! The realization made my muscles convulse with horror, but before my orgasm-addled brain managed to launch into full panic-mode, he clamped his teeth down hard around the back of my neck again.

I whimpered and went limp. It felt... very pleasant, even as my conscious mind sensed the press of his power manipulating me to surrender. But why fight it? He was so strong, so completely capable of taking care of me. Hadn't he just proven that by executing my attackers?

My nipples hardened and I moaned again, this time not from distress. He had made me feel so very good, too...

When his power withdrew again, it took my panic with it. All that was left was my desire for more. He slid his hands up underneath my coat and sweater, stroking along my bare skin, and I leaned back against his strong torso, inviting his touch to consume my entire body.

He didn't hesitate to accept. His strong body pressed in close behind me as he pushed his fingers up underneath my bra to pinch my pebbled nipples. I jerked and groaned in response, spreading my legs wider in an instinctive request to be filled.

The Shade growled against the back of my neck and his fingers constricted tighter around my stiff buds for a moment before he finally moved them lower again. I moaned, letting my hips surge forward to meet his touch when he slid both hands down over my soft stomach. One went to my pulsing clit, immediately pressing in in just the right way, while the other disappeared behind me.

"I want you to want it, kitten. Tell me you want my cock—tell me you want me to possess every inch of your soft little body," he murmured against my neck, rubbing at my tight nub of nerves until I could feel my moisture drip down my inner thighs and every nerve in my throbbing sex flame with pure *need.*

I managed a breathy "please, please, *yes,*" because there was nothing I needed more than for him to take me then and there.

That was apparently exactly what he had been waiting for.

The Shade pulled my ruined pants further down my thighs, and then something warm and *thick* pressed against my slick folds. He lined his hips up with mine, and all I could think about was how desperately I needed this—how much I needed *him.*

It didn't matter that he was evil, or that even through my lust I was still terrified of him and everything he stood for—all that mattered was that he was exactly what my body craved.

When he finally pushed in, my last connection to sanity snapped.

"Ngh!"

My ensuing cry was as much from a delicious sort of pain as it was pure pleasure, because The Shade was *big.* I whimpered as he bottomed out in that first, smooth stroke into my tight sheath, and tried to raise up on my tiptoes to escape the full penetration. His hands found my hips, pressing me down. And then he started thrusting.

"Yes!" Despite the shock of being stretched so completely and forced to take more than I ever had before, something deep and primal took over my conscience. This was exactly what I needed, what I'd always needed—to be ravaged by a man strong enough to make me submit and big enough to fill that aching, needy hollow inside of me.

"That's it, kitten. Take all of me," he rasped, and then he sank his teeth into my nape again.

I mewled in response, and my pussy clutched at his thick cock as if trying to force it to stop the long, thorough thrusts he was opening me up with. My body's instinctive protest was no match for his brutal strength, and he pushed into my core anyway with soft grunts, never altering his pace.

I slumped against the wall, biting my lip to stop myself from crying out again. Instead, my breathing came in short pants that mirrored the sharp bursts of rapture coursing through my entire body for every time The Shade forced his thick cock in.

The Shade loosened his bite slightly, nibbling delicately to tease every sensitive nerve there rather than continuing to enforce his dominance. I shivered as my pussy spasmed in response, finally easing its tight grip on his invasive girth.

"Ooh," I moaned at the small reprieve. As amazing as it felt to be fucked by something that stretched me to my limits, my body was exhausting quickly from the unaccustomed pressure. But before I managed to relax, The Shade changed his grip. One arm went around my waist again, pressing me in tight against his strong torso, while the other hand slid down over my mound and parted my lower lips before finding my swollen clit.

I jerked as his fingers pinched my sensitive nub, and yelped when he began rubbing it hard. My entire body spasmed from the sharp waves of sensation, but my pussy's desperate milking of his cock didn't stop the assault. Instead, his hips pressed in hard, slapping against my exposed ass again and again, increasing the pace for every time he bottomed out in my frantically clutching pussy.

I had thought just the strain of taking his big cock was hard. I'd been wrong. I wailed into the night and clawed at his strong arms to ease the brutal assault on my pussy, but I might as well have tried to pry off a boulder. The Shade kept me locked against his powerful form, expertly stroking my throbbing clit while fucking me mercilessly up against the wall, harder and faster for each full thrust, and there was nothing I could do but take it.

My fingernails broke on the brick wall as I clawed at it in mindless fervor, caught between trying to escape the violent fucking and needing it to never end. "Pleasure" was too mild a word to describe the wild sensations rocketing through me, but the underlying pain of being pounded with his inhuman strength was too swathed in raw endorphins to cut through. There was only him and me, only his brutal cock fucking my helpless pussy into complete and utter submission, over and over and over.

When I came, it was like an explosion of agonizing ecstasy ripping through my pelvis into my spine and through every aching muscle in my body. But The Shade didn't stop.

I whimpered pathetically when his only reaction to my suddenly lax body was to tighten his grip around me so I didn't lose my balance, the merciless pounding of his hard length into my still weakly clenching channel never slowing.

"God, please, I need a break!" All I wanted to do was to doze off on my endorphin high, but The Shade had other plans.

"No break, kitten," he growled into my ear. "I want all of you and every last drop of your pleasure."

I moaned at his words, feeling my abused pussy clutch weakly at his thick girth in response. Despite my body's obvious reaction to his demands, I didn't think I had enough strength to continue, but I wasn't given a choice. Ignoring my weak protests, The Shade pulled me closer against his strong torso, and I was once again forced to endure the deep stimulation of his pounding cock and the ruthless friction against my clit.

But after a few moments, my half-hearted resistance died. Where he had felt too big, too deep only seconds ago, his presence inside of me now started to feel good again.

With a groan of relief I closed my eyes and let him overwhelm my senses once more, giving in to the deep pulses of pleasure he drew from my tired body. Every time he drove into me, he forced me wide all the way to my very core, and I knew nothing had ever completed me the way his rough fucking did.

Soon, my body started climbing again, and I forgot that I'd ever asked him to stop.

"Yes, *yes!* More, *fuck!*" I gasped words out without registering what they were, too focused on the delicious, raw sensation from everywhere he was touching me.

It didn't take me long to reach my peak once more.

I screamed my release out as my pussy milked his pounding cock. My vision blurred, and for a moment it felt like I would pass out. Then The Shade bit down on the back of my neck again, pulling me back into my body with the sting. He grunted behind me, and his arm around my midsection constricted before I felt his cock swell inside me. His orgasm hit just as mine peaked, pulled from his body by my spasming pussy.

I slumped in his arms, resting my forehead against the wall while I slowly came down. Nothing but peace and pleasure filled my body and mind. Even the steady pulse of his semen deep inside of me felt good—soothing.

The Shade moved his hand from my clit up under my

breasts to better support my slouching figure. His bite loosened and was replaced with a few swipes of his tongue, as if to relieve any pain his rough marking might have caused. I sighed in response and tilted my head back to rest it against his broad chest, wanting more of his care. It felt so good when he nuzzled his head in against the back of mine and stroked his big hands up and down my stomach.

I felt like I was floating in a drugged daze, the only thing keeping me connected to the real world being his soft touches and the pleasant ache between my legs where our bodies were still intimately joined.

Only when he finally pulled out of me did my consciousness rear its ugly head.

The first thing that struck me was the coldness of the air pressing in against everything from my kneecaps up to my abdomen where I was bared to the elements. Next was the strong scents of sex and blood, the stickiness of the fluids dripping out of me and down my thighs, and finally the delicate soreness inside me.

"No." My broken whisper followed the sudden flood of realization. I had let the most depraved and dangerous man in the entire city fuck me in an alley, surrounded by body parts. What kind of woman would ever allow his touch, let alone *enjoy* it? As much as I wanted to claim he had forced me, forced my will to bend for his, the awful truth was engraved into my very soul.

I had wanted it. Every bit of it.

"Yes," he said, his voice completely calm and collected again, as if his semen wasn't dripping down my thighs in sticky ribbons. "You belong to me now."

I wanted to deny him, but as I leaned against the dirty brick wall I'd just spent the past half hour getting fucked against, the protest died on my lips. He had told me what letting him mark and take me would mean—and I had let him do it. The way my body still throbbed from his rough claiming didn't exactly allow for much argument.

I was his.

"Why?" I didn't want to turn around and look at him, but having my back to him left me feeling even more vulnerable than I already did. Slowly, I turned to face the man, the monster, who had taken me as his.

His scarred lip was pulled up in a wry smile. "You want to know why I claimed you? Being protected from other supes isn't enough?"

"We both know that's not why you did it." Despite my combative words, my voice caught in my throat. I coughed, annoyed with my own weakness even as I had to fight not to tremble under his gaze.

"True." The Shade reached out and pressed a finger underneath my chin. I flinched, but he caught me easily, lifting my head up to meet his unsettling eyes. "I have little interest in the safety of humans. I do, however, enjoy taking what the arrogant fool who left a half-mark on your neck thought belonged to him. He will be so very displeased."

Heat rushed to my cheeks when I realized exactly what he meant. He had claimed me, like I was an object to possess, just to piss off Lightning. If the hero even gave a damn. I don't know why I cared, but the knowledge that I was nothing but a pawn in whatever rivalry existed between the two superhumans felt like a slap to the face.

I lowered my gaze. "Can I go home now?"

The Shade loosened his grip on my chin and stepped back, giving me enough room to slip past him and out of the alley. "You may."

My fingers felt stiff and clumsy as I tried to get my ripped clothes at least somewhat in order, but after some fumbling I managed to pull up my pants and cover my private parts. I ignored the unpleasant feeling of the fluids covering my lower half and slid to my right, with my back pressed against the wall to avoid touching him or any of the body parts on the ground as I squeezed past. Only when I was certain I was past the massive bulk of his body did I turn around to face the entrance of the alleyway—and the path to my freedom.

"Kathryn."

The dark voice, strong with the air of command, made me freeze, one foot lifted mid-flight.

"Don't go looking for trouble. I will be very displeased with you if you follow anymore leads without my approval. Is that understood?"

A shudder made my back stiffen, and I could feel the weight of his stare pierce the area between my shoulder blades. I have no idea how I managed to croak a shaky *"yes"* before I fled into the night—fled the most dangerous man in the entire city.

The man who had claimed me as his.

SEVEN

I cried a lot that night, curled up in the safety of my bed while the shock of everything that had happened took control of my exhausted body. Only when the first rays of the morning sun filtered through my window did I finally run out of tears, leaving a feeling of numbness behind that finally allowed me to sleep.

The numbness was still there when I woke up in the early afternoon, along with the stiff muscles and white streaks down my thighs that reminded me all too vividly of my close encounter with St. Anthony's greatest villain.

It was while I was staring at the dried-up semen on my skin and my brain idly reminded me that I'd need to stop by the pharmacy for a pill that the numb feeling finally disappeared. Seething anger took its place.

Who the *hell* did he think he was, treating me like some disposable toy? Sure, it wasn't like I'd had the presence of mind to remember protection, but given my encounter with the thugs who'd brutalized me, I didn't think I could be blamed for having a momentary lapse in judgment. The oversized goon who'd pressed me up against a wall and fucked me into submission, on the other hand? Heck yeah, I could blame him.

The thought of his hands and cock taking control of my body made my pussy throb unexpectedly. The delicate ache, and the shame of knowing that however much I was shocked and horrified about my encounter with The Shade, the memory of it still had my body aching for more, only increased my anger. I chose to direct it at The Shade, rather than my own wanton body. And Lightning, while I was at it. If it hadn't been for his half-claim, The Shade would never have thought to mark me. The fact that I probably would be dead at the hands of the thugs if The Shade hadn't taken an interest in me was something that, for now, I chose to ignore.

Both supes were clearly involved in whatever it was I had stumbled across with my article, and I seemed to have gotten stuck in the middle of their strife. Not the best place for a human girl to be—even if it did come with mind-blowing sex.

Huffing, I got out of bed and limped to the bathroom, determined to cleanse my mind and body of the lingering fear and longing.

Yet as I stood under the hot spray of the shower, I kept thinking back to how both Lightning and The Shade had told me to "stay out of trouble." It would undoubtedly be the easier thing to do, if I trusted The Shade to keep his promise to protect me. I didn't, though. Lightning hadn't protected me when I was attacked, and The Shade... well, being the biggest, baddest villain in town didn't exactly give him the most sterling of reputations. He had marked me to get at Lightning, and I had zero expectation that I was anything but a passing amusement to him.

The mark on the back of my neck pulsed weakly, as if to chastise me for my thoughts. I rubbed it irritably, and ignored the way touching it made my nipples harden. Yeah, as much as both supes might have warned me to not go chasing this story, it seemed to me that the only chance I had at getting out of whatever rabbit hole I'd fallen into was to keep digging until I made my way out of it alive. Trusting either of the two men who had tried—and in The Shade's case, succeeded—to brand me like cattle would undoubtedly just land me in the role of a piece of rope in their tug-of-war. A piece of rope that would eventually snap.

The idea came out of nowhere. I stopped mid-shampooing, with my arms still lifted above my head and my fingers tangled in my wet locks.

If I wanted to get closer to the truth of what was going on with the superhumans and the mayor, I should look for other people who had stumbled across small pieces of the puzzle. But instead of looking for someone who had all the answers, perhaps I should look for someone who wasn't there anymore. If The Shade hadn't saved me, I would be dead. Perhaps there were other journalists out there who hadn't been so lucky.

I finished up in the shower as quickly as I could and wrapped myself in a towel, then practically sprinted to my computer, too filled with purpose to stop for clothes.

It took me less than an hour to find what I was looking for.

Back in spring, Peter Miller had written a lot of outspoken blog posts about a superhuman villain called Bright and his supposed involvement with the mayor. The last installment on his blog described a conspiracy between the two, which vaguely outlined how the mayor had shifted city resources to fund weapons used by Bright in a major bank robbery the previous December.

It sounded like the ramblings of a madman, but that blog post was dated back in May—more than four months ago. When I checked Peter's social media profiles, there hadn't been any activity since May there, either. He was gone.

I bit my lip as I scrolled through his friends list. It could have been a coincidence. He could have died of natural causes, or maybe just given up on the Internet. Or gone on a nice trip somewhere warm and sunny. As I glanced at his smiling profile picture, I hoped he had. But after having been physically attacked for my own writings concerning the mayor and the superhumans, I somehow doubted that was the case.

There. My musings stopped when I came across the profile of a young man called Aaron "The Shizz" Kempf on Peter's friends list, who had his address listed. When I scrolled through his pictures, I saw several of him and Peter together, smiling happily. He should be able to tell me if the reason for Peter's absence from the Internet had a less troubling explanation than what my gut was telling me.

And if not, then this Bright person might be my next clue.

I looked out through the Bailey Hat windows lining the entire outer wall of my loft. The sun was still out, but Aaron lived across the river. It would be dark before I got home again, and after last night...

I shivered at the memory of fleeing through empty streets from the men hunting me like an animal. I had no desire to be out in the city after dark, but I needed to know if Peter had suffered the same fate I'd almost encountered last night. At least Aaron lived in a much better part of town than the deserted industrial quarter I'd been so stupid to go traipsing through on my own.

With a determined roll of my shoulders, I shook off my sense of dread at the prospect of braving the darkened streets and went to get dressed. If I was going to get myself out of this mess, I needed to find out exactly what it was I'd stumbled across with my article.

Hiding inside my apartment forever would not help me —following my instincts might.

At least, I hoped as much.

EIGHT

THE SHADE

She was such a frail-looking little thing, what with her soft curves and short stature. So completely vulnerable in her humanity. Yet as he saw her sit nearly naked in front of her computer, the obsessive fire in her eyes was evident even through her windows. She wasn't staying out of trouble like a meek little human should—she was undoubtedly looking for more clues to the web of corruption St. Anthony was tangled in.

The Shade's mouth pulled into a wry smile, even as annoyance at being disobeyed rose in his gut. She had spine, the human, even if her physical appearance would suggest otherwise. First waltzing down dark and abandoned alleys in blind pursuit of a lead, and now *this.* While he couldn't see her screen, he had no doubt she was in the process of getting even deeper into the thick of it.

Of course, that was what he wanted—a reporter he could control, and who was invested in exposing the mayor and whatever deal he had going on with some of the higher-ups in the supe community. He had never concerned himself

A human pet to dominate and control.
To *breed*.
That's what I am to them.
They don't care what I want—they only care who wins the claim to call me his.
But with corruption running deep, and my city on the brink of destruction, I need to find a way to save it. If the two *supes* fighting for dominance over my body refuse to do it... I guess I have to.

CONNECT WITH NORA

Want to chat all things alpha? (and ruthlessly sexy book-boyfriends in general?)

JOIN NORA'S READER'S GROUP:

EMAIL:
www.nora-ash.com/newsletter

MADE & BROKEN

Dangerous

Monster

Trouble

CPSIA information can be obtained
at www.ICGtesting.com
Printed in the USA
LVHW032112310323
743149LV00005B/821

9 781913 924096